1.

Last-
Minute
Harry

The whole thing was really Mr. Onetree's fault. At least that's what Mary Rose thought.

It began because her father didn't stop for gas in time. The needle pointed to empty. Mary Rose called Mr. Onetree's attention to that fact each time they passed a gas station.

"I've told you a hundred times," Mr. Onetree said. "I can still go another ten or fifteen miles easily."

There was no use trying to talk to her father, Mary Rose knew. Mr. Onetree never took care of anything until the very last minute. When it came time to pay his taxes, he stood in line at the post office to get his letter mailed just before the midnight deadline. When he had to get new license plates, he always wound up on the last day of the month at the end of the line that went around the block.

Mrs. Onetree called him "Last-Minute Harry."

Mr. Onetree had waited till the last minute to take Mary Rose and her sister Jo-Beth, who was asleep on the back seat of the car, to stay with Aunt Madge.

"It's beginning to snow," Mrs. Onetree had warned her husband. "I'd like to see Mary Rose and Jo-Beth settled in with Madge before I go to the hospital." Before Mr. Onetree could answer, she went on, "I'm the one who's having the baby, Harry. So don't tell me there's lots of time."

"I don't see why we need another baby around here," Jo-Beth had said. "I think two girls in the family are plenty." Jo-Beth had liked the idea of going to visit Aunt Madge, who had just moved to Indianapolis, but she didn't think she should be pushed out of her own house because a new baby was coming. It would probably be a boy, anyway, because that's what her father kept hoping it would be, and then there

Help!
I'm a Prisoner
in the Library

Help!
I'm a Prisoner in the Library
Eth Clifford

Illustrated by George Hughes

HOUGHTON MIFFLIN COMPANY BOSTON 1979

For information about permission to reproduce selections from this book,
write to Permissions, Houghton Mifflin Company,
215 Park Avenue South, New York, New York 10003.

www.houghtonmifflinbooks.com

Library of Congress Cataloging-in-Publication Data
Clifford, Eth, 1915-
Help! I'm a prisoner in the library.

SUMMARY: Two girls spend an adventurous night trapped
inside the public library during a terrible blizzard.
[1. Libraries—Fiction. 2. Blizzards—Fiction]
I. Title.
PZ7.C62214He   [Fic]   79-14447
ISBN 0-395-28478-3 (hardcover)   0-618-49482-0 (pbk.)

Manufactured in the United States of America
MP 10 9 8 7 6 5 4 3 2 1

Contents

For my good friends the librarians

They spun a web of golden words
    And held me fast therein—
A lonely child, who learned from them
    Where magic could begin.

would be a lot of fuss over it. "Wait and see," she told Mary Rose darkly.

"You'll probably have a *boy*," Jo-Beth had said, getting what her mother called "that gloomy Gus" look on her face.

"And we'll probably all be standing here till doomsday," Mrs. Onetree had answered impatiently, trying to push her family out the door.

"I'll drop them off and come right back," Mr. Onetree had promised. "As soon as I can, anyway. I figure a good two hours there and another two hours back."

"You're not to speed. Mary Rose, make sure your father doesn't speed. And you watch that gas gauge, too. When it's down to a quarter of a tank, you remind your father to stop at a gas station. Don't let him wait till the last minute. I know I can depend on you, Mary Rose," her mother had said.

So Mary Rose had watched the gauge, and she had reminded her father when the needle moved way down below the quarter-tank mark. But it hadn't helped. And now here they were, pulled over to the curb, on some strange corner in Indianapolis. Mary Rose was surprised the car hadn't stopped dead right in the middle of the street.

Jo-Beth woke up. "Are we there yet?" She rubbed the car window. "I can't see out. Why are we just sitting here?"

"We're out of gas," Mary Rose said in her best I-told-you-so voice. "And it's snowing harder."

"You girls sit tight." Mr. Onetree started to jump out of the car. "I'm going to get the gas can from the trunk and jog over to that gas station we passed a few blocks back. Remember, stay in the car and keep the doors locked. I'll be back in a couple of minutes."

"We'll freeze," Jo-Beth said with satisfaction. "The snow will come down and cover the car and we'll freeze to death while you're gone."

Mr. Onetree shook his head. How could two sisters be so different? They looked very much alike, with their fine straight brown hair and dark brown eyes and their bright smiles (except that Jo-Beth's smile showed a tooth missing in front). Mary Rose was a practical-minded girl.

Responsible, that's what Mary Rose was. Jo-Beth, on the other hand, made a big deal out of everything. She could dramatize the smallest happening.

Freeze to death! Mr. Onetree shook his head again. "Cover yourself with the blanket if you get cold. And remember, keep the doors locked."

The minute Mr. Onetree was out of sight, Jo-Beth announced, "I have to go to the bathroom."

"Why didn't you say something before? You could have gone to the gas station with Daddy."

"I didn't have to go then. I have to go now." Jo-Beth added, "It's an emergency."

"You're just like Daddy. Everything at the

last minute. You'll just have to hold back."

"I can't hold back. It's an *emergency*, Mary Rose."

Mary Rose sighed. "Well, maybe someone will let us in someplace. Come on."

The two girls got out of the car. Mary Rose squinted her eyes half-closed to keep the snow and the rising wind from cutting off her vision.

"There's a building down the street. They probably have a bathroom. Come on, Jo-Beth. Walk fast. It's cold."

The snow was settling; walking was a struggle. Jo-Beth held her head down because the wind was nipping her cheeks and nose. Mary Rose kept staring ahead so she could see how much farther they had to go. So it was Mary Rose who spotted the sign in front of a huge old house not far from the corner:

THE FINTON MEMORIAL LIBRARY

FOR CHILDREN

HOURS 9 TO 5 DAILY

Mary Rose pushed her sleeve back so she could see her watch. It would be five o'clock in about five minutes.

"Quick, Jo-Beth," she shouted at her sister. "We can go in here. It's a library. They always have a bathroom in the library."

The girls hurried up the steps which led to a wide stone porch that seemed to wrap itself around the front and sides of the house. Set back on the porch were two wide doors. The lower half of the doors was made of light and dark pieces of wood set so they formed a diamond pattern. Smaller pieces of wood in the same design held large glass panels in place on the upper half of the doors. The glass seemed to have waves in it, like small ripples in a pond.

When Mary Rose pushed the door open, the girls found themselves standing in an entry way.

"At least it's warm in here," Jo-Beth said, brushing the snow from her jacket and jeans.

"Look at this floor! I never saw one like this before," said Mary Rose. The floor was made of mosaic—soft-colored blue and gray chips of stone that had been laid in place by hand, piece by piece.

"It has pictures in it."

Jo-Beth didn't care about pictures in a floor. She was busy opening another door in the entry.

Like the front door, this, too, was half wood and half glass.

"This isn't a library," Jo-Beth said. "This is somebody's house."

"No, it isn't. Look at all the books." There were books everywhere—on shelves, on tables, on carts, and on a large desk which Mary Rose guessed must belong to the librarian.

The room the girls were standing in was quite large. Mary Rose had to lean her head way back to see the high decorated ceiling. The rich brown wood walls glowed in the light of an enormous crystal chandelier hanging in the center of the room. The chandelier had tiny glass droplets that made a slight tinkling sound caused by the breeze that had whistled in when the girls had opened the front door.

They could see other rooms through a number of arched doorways. To their right, toward the back of the house, a wide, handsome stairway turned and twisted to an upper floor. The steps were covered with dark red carpeting. Across the bottom step, stretching from one banister to the other, was a black velvet twisted rope. In the middle of the rope was a sign with the words *Private. No admittance to the public.*

It was very, very quiet. There was no one in the room, not even a librarian.

"Where is everybody?" Jo-Beth asked in a hushed voice.

"Who'd come out in this kind of weather to go to the library?" Mary Rose demanded. "Except us. Because of you and your emergencies."

"But where's the librarian?" Jo-Beth insisted.

"She's probably looking in all the rooms to make sure everybody's gone before she locks up and goes home," Mary Rose explained. She looked around. "It sure is different. Hey! Jo-Beth! Look back there. That looks like some funny old kind of wagon in that back room. With people sitting in it." Mary Rose sounded excited. "Come on. Let's go see what it is."

Jo-Beth wasn't interested. When Mary Rose mentioned the emergency, she suddenly remembered why they were here. She caught sight of the sign that said "rest room." An arrow pointed to the back of the house.

"I really have to *go!*" Jo-Beth warned.

As Mary Rose walked to the back with her sister, she thought, "I wish we had time to see if that really is a wagon with people in it. I wish we had lots and lots of time to stay here. I bet there are all kinds of interesting things to see in those other rooms . . ."

"You crossed your fingers and closed your eyes. You made a *wish*," Jo-Beth said knowingly as she rushed into the rest room.

Mary Rose followed her sister with dragging steps. "Maybe I can take a quick look on the way out," she told herself. "Just one quick look before the librarian makes us leave."

2.

The
Spooky Blue
Lights

Mary Rose made a quick decision.

"I have to see that wagon," she told her sister. "Meet me in that back room."

Without waiting for a reply, she ran off.

When Jo-Beth finally joined her, Mary Rose had already examined the display.

"It's a school bus," she explained. "From long ago. Only then it was called a 'kid hack.'"

"A *what?*"

"A 'kid hack.' And those big dolls sitting up there are dressed just the way the kids dressed in olden times."

"They look more like the store dummies you see in windows. Look at the way they're arranged, Mary Rose."

11

Two of the dolls appeared to be leaning slightly out of the wagon, as if they were watching the road. Two had their heads turned toward each other; they almost seemed to be having a conversation. Three sat one behind another, their eyes straight ahead.

"What does the sign say?" Jo-Beth asked eagerly.

Her sister read it aloud:

Early school buses were called kid hacks. They were ordinary wagons covered with either sailcloth or canvas; the students being taken to and from school sat on hard wooden benches. In bad weather, sailcloth curtains were dropped to protect the children from rain or snow or wind.

In winter, the wagons were heated by small stoves in which coal or wood or even corncobs were burned. Sometimes the stove was fastened in place under the floor of the kid hack. In some wagons, the small black stove was placed inside.

Later models were much fancier. Rubber tires replaced the wooden wheels; real glass windows were used instead of cloth curtains. Some kid hacks even boasted carpeting on the floor and lap robes to keep the children comfortable against the wintry blasts.

As Mary Rose read, Jo-Beth went around to the back of the display. Now she called, "There's a little stove in the wagon. And more old clothes on a bench."

Mary Rose went behind the display, too. She picked up some dried corncobs from the wagon floor and put them into the claw-footed little iron stove while Jo-Beth held a dress against herself, wondering if it would fit.

Neither of the girls heard the librarian moving about. And Vilmor Finton, the librarian, didn't realize anyone else was in the library. No one had come after it had begun to snow. Miss

13

Finton had almost decided to close up early, but the sign outside listed the hours as 9 to 5 daily. Miss Finton was a woman who believed in carrying out her duties.

There were ten rooms downstairs—Grandfather Finton had always said that when he built a house, he built it *big*—and Miss Finton had been going from room to room. She did this each evening at closing time to make sure everyone was out of the building. She had looked into the rest room. Now she went to the room with the kid hack display. She often found children lingering here. She didn't bother to go into the room, just stood at the doorway and glanced inside quickly. Both girls were hidden from her view by the kid hack, and since Mary Rose and Jo-Beth had stopped talking for the moment, Miss Finton didn't hear anything, either. Satisfied, she walked away, and headed for the outside front doors.

Just as she was about to lock them, a man rapped sharply on the window. Miss Finton opened the door the merest crack, but even so snow began to whirl in.

"Yes. What is it?" Miss Finton asked impatiently.

"Excuse me. Are there two little girls in here by any chance? One is ten and the other is seven . . ."

"The library is closed."

"They might be in the bathroom," the man pleaded. "Please. Will you just let me come in and look?"

Miss Finton had read many stories in the newspapers about people who came to one's door and asked to use the phone or made up excuses about accidents or whatever. Once inside, they attacked anyone foolish enough to let them in.

Miss Finton lived alone and liked it. And she wasn't afraid of staying in this big old house by herself. Just the same, she wasn't going to let this man put one foot inside the door. To begin with, Miss Finton had already checked the bathroom and the other rooms downstairs. She *knew* the building was empty, except for herself, of course. Furthermore, this man's eyes were wild. He was breathing hard. And his voice was shaky.

"There are no children here," Miss Finton insisted, and she closed the door firmly in Mr. Onetree's face. Then she locked and bolted the outside front doors and did the same with the inner doors. Miss Finton didn't believe in taking unnecessary chances. The double-locked doors, both inside and out, could be opened only with her keys.

Going back to the stairway, she stepped over the sign and walked briskly up the steps.

Miss Finton did everything briskly. She was about medium height. Her lively black eyes exactly matched her black hair, which was short and thick and bristled up from her head like the fur on an angry cat.

Her hands seemed almost too large for her body, but Miss Finton was proud of them. They were good strong hands, and they served her very well.

At the top of the landing, Miss Finton took one last look at the floor below. Then she turned and went up another stairway that led to the third floor. Miss Finton always checked the windows upstairs to make sure they were locked.

Satisfied that all was well, she went down

again to the second floor, where she pressed a switch that turned off the big bright lights below. She pressed another switch that turned on small dim blue lights in each of the rooms downstairs, and on the landing.

When the lights went out so suddenly, the two girls were so shocked they couldn't speak. Jo-Beth gave a small gasp. Mary Rose realized two things almost at once. They had forgotten all about the time. And they had forgotten about their father, who must have come back to the car with the gas by now.

"The librarian's gone home. I'll bet she locked us in!" Mary Rose nodded her head. "And Daddy doesn't even know where we are. And all because of you and your last-minute emergencies." She glared at her sister. "See what you've gone and done to us."

"Me? *Me?* Who wanted to come in and take a look at this old wagon? Who was the one that made the secret wish?" Jo-Beth shivered. "I don't like these spooky blue lights. They make everything so weird."

Mary Rose agreed. The big dolls in their strange clothes suddenly made her feel uneasy. Were the dolls moving? Weren't they getting bigger? Mary Rose felt scared. This was exactly the way she had felt the time her father had taken them to the wax museum.

"They're creepy," Jo-Beth whispered, almost as if she could read her sister's mind. "The way they keep staring. It's like they see something we can't. I *hate* these blue lights!" Even Mary Rose's face was beginning to look spooky in the dim-colored room. "I'm getting out of here!"

Jo-Beth dropped the dress she had been holding when the lights went out. She wanted to run, but it was hard to see where she was going. She came out from behind the display and crept along to the front door, with Mary Rose right behind her. At the door, she pulled and tugged at the knob.

"What good is that? The doors are locked."

"There she goes again, Miss Know-It-All," Jo-Beth thought, irritated. She could see now that there was no use trying to get the doors open. But it made her feel as if she was doing something. "I know they're locked," she snapped. "I thought maybe I could loosen them up or something." She was so angry she kicked the door. "Whoever heard of locking a door *inside* with a key?"

"Maybe she has a lot of valuable things here. I'd do the same if I had something valuable," Mary Rose said thoughtfully.

Jo-Beth turned and stood with her back up against the door. The blue lights were even worse in here because the room was so big. Shadows crouched down from the walls and moved closer and closer. Jo-Beth swallowed hard, but the hollow sensation in her stomach refused to go away.

Outside, the wind was tearing at the house, moaning and screaming, trying to get inside. Jo-Beth was sure the wind was calling her name in a long, drawn-out shriek—*Jo–Be-e-e-eth! Jo–Be-e-e-eth!*

She couldn't stand it anymore.

"Oh, Mary Rose," she sobbed. "We're never going to get out of here. The librarian's gone, and Daddy doesn't know where we are. Suppose it storms for days and days? We'll starve. They'll find our poor starved bodies . . ." Jo-Beth became so interested in what she was saying that she stopped crying. Wouldn't everybody be sad? And the new baby would never know what wonderful sisters he had had, especially Jo-Beth.

"No wonder Mommy calls you 'gloomy Gus,'" said Mary Rose. "You're so silly." She started to walk away from the door.

Jo-Beth promptly followed. "I don't want to stay here by myself. Where are you going?"

"I'm going to find the phone, dummy. You said at least one sensible thing. Nobody knows we're here. So I guess it would be a good idea to call somebody on the phone and tell them where we are."

3.
"Off
With Their
Heads"

"Who are you going to call?" Jo-Beth asked when Mary Rose finally found the phone. It was hidden on a shelf just below the sign that read

CHECK BOOKS OUT HERE.

"Dumb old place for a phone," Mary Rose said in an angry voice.

"Maybe the librarian is a little old lady who can't reach higher than that," Jo-Beth said. "Maybe she's a midget, or an elf..."

"Now don't you start in again with that kind of stuff," her sister warned. "You and your imagination."

Jo-Beth didn't care what Mary Rose said about her imagination. She liked the idea of a tiny elfin librarian, dressed in green, with a green pointed cap topped by a small bell, sitting on ahigh stool, checking out books.

Mary Rose had started to dial a number.

"Call Aunt Madge. Tell her to come and get us right away."

"Don't start telling me what to do." Mary Rose was still out of sorts. "Aunt Madge only just moved to Indianapolis. She hasn't got a phone yet."

"Well then, call Daddy or Mommy. I don't *like* this place."

Mary Rose didn't pay any attention. She had dialed the operator, and a voice was already speaking to her at the other end. Mary Rose said, "I want to call Fort Wayne collect." She gave the operator her home number and her mother's name.

"I want to talk to Mommy. Give me the phone," Jo-Beth said.

Mary Rose pushed Jo-Beth's hand away. She listened to the voice on the phone, and then she hung up. She pulled at her lower lip with her thumb and forefinger.

"Something's wrong," Jo-Beth said quickly. When Mary Rose started folding her lip that way, she was good and worried.

"The operator says the phones are down in Fort Wayne. On account of the blizzard."

"What's a blizzard?" Jo-Beth asked.

"It's a terrible snowstorm. *Mountains* of snow. And gusty winds." That's what they always said on TV in the weather reports. "Gusty winds."

"You're just making that up," Jo-Beth wailed.

"I don't make things up. That's what a blizzard is."

"It is not. You just like to scare me. You're really mean!" Jo-Beth moved away from her sister.

"The operator said the blizzard was everywhere. Come on over to the window so we can look out and see it," Mary Rose said more kindly.

At one of the front windows facing out on the porch, the two girls rubbed the wet panes and tried to peer out. It was night—darkness came early in the winter. Still, the falling snow brightened the world outside, especially when the street lights gleamed on the twirling flakes.

A car went by, moving slowly, and then another. Two young boys hurried past, walking backward, hunching their heads into their jackets to protect themselves against the wind.

The sisters knocked and knocked on the window, but the boys didn't even look their way.

"It's no use," Mary Rose said. "They can't hear us. We're too far from the sidewalk."

"I know," Jo-Beth cried. "I'll make a sign and put it up on the window."

"You can if you want to. I'm going to call the police."

Jo-Beth ran back to the librarian's desk. She pulled drawers open until she found what she was looking for—a big sheet of paper, a thick black marking pen, and some Scotch tape. Meanwhile, Mary Rose picked up the phone.

"Operator," she said, "I want the police."

"Help!" Jo-Beth started to print.

"Are you in trouble?" the operator asked. She sounded suspicious.

"Yes, we are. Please. I want the police."

"How do you spell prisoner?" Jo-Beth asked.

"Just how it sounds. Don't bother me now, Jo-Beth. This is important."

"So is this," Jo-Beth said. "Come on, Mary Rose. You know I'm a terrible speller."

A voice in Mary Rose's ear came on so quickly that she couldn't catch what the man said—mumble, mumble, precinct, mumble, mumble Johnson. He spoke just as Mary Rose was saying to her sister, "Put down p–r–i–s–o–n . . ."

"Who is this?" the voice asked.

". . .e–r," Mary Rose finished quickly. "Is this the police?"

Jo-Beth shouted into the phone. "We're prisoners! We're prisoners in the library!"

"You kids stop playing with your phone," the officer scolded. "We have to keep all these lines open for emergencies." He slammed the receiver down so hard it made Mary Rose's ear tingle.

"Are they coming to get us?"

"He hung up on me. He didn't even want to *listen*."

Mary Rose didn't know that at that very moment, Sergeant Johnson was grumbling, "That's the fifth nutty call I've had in the last fifteen minutes. This one was something else. Some little kid yelling she was a prisoner. In the library yet!"

Mary Rose wasn't a girl to give up easily. She lifted the receiver again.

"How do you spell library?" Jo-Beth was busy with her sign.

"I can't talk to you and talk on the phone at the same time. Just spell it! And leave me alone! Hello, operator? I want the fire department."

Jo-Beth, meanwhile, was finishing her sign. It looked fine to her. In big letters, she had printed:

"Now to hang it up in the window," Jo-Beth thought. A sign was better than a phone call. People believed signs.

Mary Rose was having a problem.

"Aren't you the same little girl who just asked for the police?"

"Yes, but they hung up on me."

"Is your mother there?" the operator asked. When Mary Rose said no, the operator wanted to know, "Is your father there?"

"He went out to get gas. See, he waited until the tank was empty . . ."

"Is there any grownup in the house at all?" the operator interrupted.

"That's what I'm trying to tell you." Why didn't people *listen?* "Nobody's here except me and my little sister. We're locked up in the . . ."

Without warning, the phone went dead. No sound came from it at all, not even a hum or a dial tone. At the same time, the lights went out and the room was swallowed up in darkness.

Jo-Beth called from the window in panic, "The lights just went off in the street." She started to run toward her sister. Mary Rose could hear her banging into things as she tried to find her way back to the librarian's desk and Mary Rose.

The two girls crouched behind the desk.

"I wish the blue lights would come back on," Jo-Beth whispered. "They were spooky, but they were better than nothing."

"The power line must be down." Mary Rose didn't feel nearly as brave as she sounded. But she was ten and her sister was only seven. "Stop shaking, Jo-Beth. Just think of it this way. We can't get out. But nobody can get in, either. So we're perfectly safe."

Jo-Beth relaxed a little. "I wouldn't mind it so much if it wasn't so dark."

Even at home, with the whole family there, Jo-Beth liked to have a small lamp on all night. *Things* came out at you in the night, when everyone was asleep, but not so long as there was the tiniest bit of light in the room.

"Maybe I can find a flashlight in one of these drawers." Mary Rose ran her fingers across the desk and down one side. She pulled a drawer open and slid her hand around inside. Pencils, small pads of paper, paper clips—wait a minute. What was this? It felt like, it smelled like, chocolate. A candy bar!

"I'm starved. We never had supper," Mary Rose said.

"So am I. But we'd better not eat it. It could be poisoned." Jo-Beth could hardly wait to tear off the wrapper. "I'll taste it first," she offered nobly. "Just in case it is. Poisoned."

"Can't you ever stop play-acting? Why would a librarian keep poisoned candy in her desk? Honestly, Jo-Beth."

While she was talking, she continued her search. In the very last drawer, she found a key ring with a tiny flashlight attached to it.

"What can you see with that?"

Mary Rose didn't bother to answer. Who could ever satisfy Jo-Beth? She was just about to ask her sister for her half of the candy bar when, without warning, her hand was seized and Jo-Beth's nails were digging hard into her flesh.

"I heard something weird." Jo-Beth had her lips against her sister's ear. "Sh-h-h! Listen. Something is flying around in here. Something big."

Jo-Beth was right. Mary Rose could hear it now, too. Whatever it was, it was making a strange rushing noise fairly close by.

"Bats!" Jo-Beth screamed.

At the same time, a harsh voice demanded, "What's your name, child? What's your name?"

Jo-Beth tried to disappear under the desk. "Bats," she repeated in terror.

"Bats don't talk." Mary Rose licked her lips and swallowed. She forgot about the flashlight in her hands. Turning toward where she thought the voice was coming from, she replied, "I'm Mary Rose. And this is my little sister Jo-Beth."

"Don't talk to it," Jo-Beth begged.

"Off with their heads," the same harsh voice ordered. "Off with their heads." The voice seemed to be moving away. Mary Rose knelt beside her sister. "Keep down. I'm going to turn on the flashlight and see who's talking."

"No. Don't. I don't want to see it."

But Mary Rose had already pressed the "on" button. She began to giggle. "It's a bird, Jo-Beth. Come on. You can look now. It's a mynah bird."

"Like the one in the pet shop?"

The bird ruffled its feathers. Its head to one side, it remarked, "Say how do you do."

"How do you do?" Jo-Beth grinned. Without thinking, she began to eat her sister's half of the candy bar. When she realized what she was doing, her face turned red. "Oh, Mary Rose. I'm sorry!"

She didn't know what Mary Rose was going to say because at that exact moment, there was a heavy thud over their heads, as if someone had fallen down.

The moaning started almost at once.

4.

The Awful
Quiet Dark
Emptiness

Jo-Beth grabbed her sister so hard that Mary Rose dropped the flashlight.

"Don't keep doing that!" Mary Rose exclaimed. She dropped to her knees and started to fumble about on the floor for the flashlight.

"You said we were safe because the door was locked. You said nobody could get in. Well, *something* got in." Jo-Beth sounded as though she blamed Mary Rose for the thump, the bump, and the moaning.

"There was no use arguing," Mary Rose thought. She began to pull at her lip. She had a big decision to make, and her sister was no help at all. The question was—should they hide downstairs, or should they go upstairs and see who—or what—was there?

The best place to hide, of course, would be in the room with the kid hack. Better still, she and Jo-Beth could dress up in the old clothes and sit inside the hack, even though the idea of sitting down beside the dolls made her skin feel crawly.

"Mary Rose." Jo-Beth's voice dropped down so low Mary Rose could hardly hear what she was saying. "Let's hide until morning." There she went again, reading Mary Rose's mind.

"What's your name?" the mynah bird croaked suddenly. "What's your name, child?"

"Why don't you just shut up, you dumb, stupid old thing?" Jo-Beth demanded.

Quickly, Mary Rose explained about going back to the kid hack room. Jo-Beth liked the idea, especially the dressing-up part. Mary Rose pressed the on button and pointed the tiny light straight ahead. Then they tiptoed across the room, being careful not to bump into anything on the way. They didn't want the thing upstairs to hear them.

The mynah bird flew beside them, its wings fanning them with cool air.

"If that bird says one more thing, I'll kill him," Jo-Beth said.

"He's supposed to talk. He's a mynah . . ."

Jo-Beth stopped walking so suddenly Mary Rose ran right into her. "I wish you would cut it out right now. Being sensible. Why do you have to be so sensible all the time?"

"I'm not going to change in the middle of the night in the middle of a library in the middle of no place just because you're such a scaredy cat," Mary Rose replied in an angry voice.

"That's not fair. You're never fair. I can't help being scared. This is a scary place."

"You can be scared and sensible, too. Don't you think I'm scared? But I'm not a big baby like you."

"If I was ten and you were only seven, I'd be nicer than you, Mary Rose. I would take care of my little sister and not pick on her all the time."

Mary Rose sighed. "You think it's easy to be the oldest? I wish we could change places just once. Then you'd see."

Jo-Beth was astonished. Didn't Mary Rose get to stay up later because she was older? Didn't she get a bigger allowance? And when Jo-Beth got mad and yelled at Mary Rose, didn't their mother always take Mary Rose's side?

36

"Don't you think I ever get tired of having Mommy or Daddy tell me to take care of you all the time?" Mary Rose continued.

"Take care of *me?*" Jo-Beth was insulted. "I'm seven years old!" She suddenly hissed in her sister's ear, the argument forgotten, "Sh-h-h! Listen! It's starting again!"

Mary Rose had heard it, too—that loud moan from upstairs. "Quick," she said, as they went into the kid hack room. She shone the tiny light so they could find their way behind the display. There the two girls undressed rapidly. Jo-Beth threw her clothes down in a heap on the floor, but Mary Rose folded each garment as she took it off and placed it neatly on one of the benches.

As soon as they had the old-fashioned dresses on, they took turns looking at each other in the small glow from the flashlight.

"This dress feels kind of nice." Jo-Beth was surprised. "Do you like yours?" Without waiting for an answer, she went on, "Let's put on one of these hats."

"It's not a hat. It's a bonnet."

Jo-Beth rolled her eyes heavenward. Mary

Rose was probably right. She almost always was right about one thing or another. But she just wished Mary Rose would keep it to herself once in a while.

"Where shall we sit?" Jo-Beth asked.

Mary Rose studied the kid hack. There was one empty bench, right up in front. "Let's sit together, up there." She'd never admit it to Jo-Beth, but Mary Rose wanted the comfort of her sister's warm body right next to her. Jo-Beth sat next to the window, or what would have been the window if the kid hack had had glass in it. Mary Rose smoothed her dress and took the seat beside her sister. The mynah bird perched on top of the wagon.

The silence was absolute. Neither sister spoke. Even the bird was quiet. Jo-Beth wanted to turn her head and look back at the dolls. She could tell Mary Rose felt the same way. After a few minutes, Jo-Beth said out of the side of her mouth, "They're *doing* something back there. I think they're moving around."

Mary Rose clutched at the flashlight so hard her knuckles began to turn white.

"They're dummies," she hissed. "They *can't* move."

"Turn the light on and let's look." Jo-Beth couldn't bear not knowing. And neither could Mary Rose. She turned on the flashlight. Slowly, very slowly, the girls peered back over their shoulders. The light shone directly on the glassy eyes of the dolls. Jo-Beth gasped. She knew it! Those glittering eyes were fixed on her. They were hard and unfriendly.

"I'm getting out of here," Jo-Beth whispered.

The mynah bird flew down and landed on one of the dolls. "Off with their heads." It nipped at the doll's bonnet, which slipped off, taking with it the wig underneath. The bald head looked menacing.

Jo-Beth jumped down from the wagon, her sister following right on her heels. The mynah bird flew along with them.

"I wish we could turn him into a flying carpet, and fly right out of here," Jo-Beth whispered. "I hate this place. I'm never going to come back. If we ever get out."

Mary Rose just held her sister's hand and led

her back to the librarian's desk. It seemed to her the safest place to hide for the moment.

When they were under the desk, she told her sister to be quiet. Mary Rose listened hard, turning her head from side to side. The moaning had stopped again. But that didn't mean that whatever was up there was gone.

"I have to know," she thought. It was the same sensation she had had in the kid hack, when she had had to put the light on and turn around and see what those dolls were doing. Knowing was bad, but not knowing was worse.

She took a deep breath. "Jo-Beth, you can stay here if you want to, but I'm going upstairs and see what's up there."

Jo-Beth put out her hand as if to stop Mary Rose. She wanted to plead with Mary Rose not to leave her. But she knew what Mary Rose was like once she made up her mind about something.

"I'm going to sit right here on the floor," Jo-Beth said. Mary Rose shrugged. She began to walk away, toward the steps. "Wait," Jo-Beth cried. "You've got the light."

Mary Rose shrugged again. She beamed the light at the sign and then up at the stairway. She took another deep breath, closing her eyes for a moment. Stepping over the sign, she put one hand on the banister and held on to the flashlight with the other. She didn't say a word when Jo-Beth raced after her, breathing hard.

"Let me walk in front of you. Please, Mary Rose. I'd rather have you right in back of me than . . ." Her voice trailed off, but Mary Rose knew exactly what her sister meant because she could feel the awful quiet dark emptiness pressing in behind her.

5.

The Body
on The
Floor

Mary Rose had once had a dream that she and
her mother and father and sister had moved to a
strange city. In the dream, her mother drove her
to a tall building and dropped her in front.
"Hurry, Mary Rose," her mother said. "Hurry.
Hurry. Hurry."

Mary Rose floated across the sidewalk. "Flying is faster than walking," she told another
child who appeared out of nowhere and was flying toward the building, too. When Mary Rose
entered the building, she couldn't fly anymore.
Someone pointed at her and then pointed up a
stairway. Mary Rose climbed and climbed.
Every time she came to a landing, someone
pointed to more steps. The more steps she
climbed, the more there were.

She might have been climbing still if Jo-Beth hadn't shaken her awake. "You're having a nightmare," Jo-Beth had bellowed in her ear. It surprised Mary Rose that she hadn't become permanently deaf.

Holding on to the banister and practically pushing Jo-Beth ahead of her step by step, Mary Rose felt as if she had somehow drifted back into that nightmare. "Maybe I just ought to wave my arms in the air and start flying," she thought to herself.

Halfway up there was a broad landing. Jo-Beth stopped abruptly, so abruptly that Mary Rose ran into her and cracked her jaw on Jo-Beth's head.

"Don't ever do that again," Mary Rose said angrily. "I think you broke my jaw."

"Something's standing over near the window." The way Jo-Beth spoke, Mary Rose was ready for some new horror. Cautiously, she flashed the light toward the window. Then she sighed. "It's a wonder you didn't turn my hair white," she scolded. That's what Mrs. Onetree always said when she was upset. Mrs. Onetree had the same fine brown hair that her daughters had, but she was always sure it was going to turn white overnight. Now Mary Rose knew what her mother meant. "It's just some kind of figure."

"What's it doing here anyway? What kind of a library is this? I'll tell you one thing, Mary Rose. I'm not going up any more steps. If we do, it will be to our certain death." Jo-Beth liked the sound of that. She repeated it with joyful gloom. "Certain death."

"Great. Just great. That's what I love about you, Jo-Beth. You really know how to cheer a person up." She moved closer to the figure. Then she laughed. "Come and see what scared you. Come on!"

Jo-Beth edged a little closer. "I know who that is. That's . . ."

". . . Pinocchio."

". . . Pinocchio," Jo-Beth finished. She giggled. "Look at the branch growing at the end of his nose. And the bird sitting on the branch and singing."

At the foot of the carved wooden figure, a small sign explained

WHENEVER PINOCCHIO TOLD A LIE,
HIS NOSE GREW LONGER AND LONGER

Jo-Beth would have settled for staying on the landing, but Mary Rose was determined to complete the journey to the second floor.

"Wait for me." Jo-Beth got in front of her sister again. As she did so, the mynah bird flew past, screaming, "Yoo-hoo! Vilmor! Vilmor!"

"Dumb, stupid bird," Jo-Beth muttered. "Why can't you just be normal like other birds and sing?"

Before long, the girls reached the head of the stairway and another wide landing, which turned around on both sides into two spacious hallways. In each hallway were a number of doors. At the farthest end on the right, a door was open. A light flickered from somewhere inside the room.

"Come on," Mary Rose said.

Jo-Beth held back. "You go first. You're older than I am. And bigger. And you have the flashlight. You could use it as a weapon if you have to."

Mary Rose looked down at the key ring and the tiny flashlight attached. She didn't bother answering. She just sighed and began to walk along the hallway. Jo-Beth stayed where she was, clutching the railing at the top step.

Mary Rose looked back. "Aren't you coming?" she demanded.

Jo-Beth shook her head.

"What are you afraid of?" Mary Rose snapped. "I've got this great big weapon, remember?"

The truth was, Mary Rose didn't want to explore by herself. Jo-Beth wasn't much help, but she was a warm, living, human body.

She waited while Jo-Beth inched her way slowly to her side. Standing as close to one another as they could, they advanced steadily toward the room with the light.

Mary Rose peered in through the open doorway. She saw a large room, comfortably furnished, with a fire glowing in a large fireplace. That was the flickering light they had seen. Not too far from the fireplace was a huge birdcage. The mynah bird was already inside, sitting on a long wooden perch, preening its feathers.

The two girls walked into the room, looking about curiously.

"Somebody lives here," Jo-Beth said finally. "I didn't know anybody ever lived in a library."

"That's what we must have heard, Jo-Beth. We must have heard the librarian. She must have knocked something over." Mary Rose's eyes began to shine with excitement. "Do you realize what this means?"

"We can get something to eat!" Jo-Beth felt relaxed enough now to remember that she was starved.

"It means we can get out!" Mary Rose felt wonderful. "If the librarian lives here, she can let us out. We're not locked in anymore."

"Well, where is she? I still don't see anybody."

"There's another door over there, in the back of the room. I'll bet she's in there. Let's go see."

Jo-Beth didn't mind. She felt braver now because there was nothing strange about this room. It was like their living room at home, only bigger, and this one had a fireplace. The fire crackled; small tongues of flame leaped upward. A large china cat was stretched out on the hearth. Ivy spilled from an iron kettle on the shelf above the fireplace, and books were scattered on the shelf as well, some held in place by bookends, some just lying in small piles. An easy chair was pulled up near the fireplace. On a table beside the chair was a beautiful silver candlestick with carved figures in the base. It held a most unusual candle, shaped like a woman with long flowing hair. She held a tiny lamb.

"Look at that!" Jo-Beth wanted to go over and run her fingers up and down the candlestick and candle, but Mary Rose was anxious to find the librarian. She motioned toward the door with her head. Once again, Jo-Beth went first, with Mary Rose trailing her. They had just walked to the far side of the long sofa, which was turned so that it faced the fireplace, when Jo-Beth came to a quick halt. Mary Rose cracked her jaw again.

"You're just doing that on purpose," Mary Rose began but she stopped talking when she saw what Jo-Beth was staring at.

There was a body on the floor—a woman.

"Is she dead?" Jo-Beth's voice trembled. "She looks dead."

"I guess we've found the librarian." Mary Rose sounded calm, but she had a funny, twisty feeling inside. She wished now that they had stayed downstairs. A dead body was a whole lot worse than even the dolls in the kid hack.

The two girls knelt down to take a closer look. With the fire behind them, their faces were shadowed and almost invisible under the peaks of the bonnets they were wearing.

It was at that moment that Vilmor Finton opened her eyes. She saw two small figures dressed exactly like the dolls in the hack, bending over her in absolute unmoving silence.

"Oh dear God," she gasped. "They've come to life."

And she promptly fainted.

6.

We
Weren't
Dead

"What does she mean, we've come to life?" Jo-Beth demanded. "We weren't dead."

"It must be these clothes. I guess it was a shock, waking up and seeing us dressed like this, after not expecting to see anybody in the house at all," Mary Rose explained. "I bet she tripped over this little iron cat. See? It's over on its side . . ."

"Like the one near the fireplace?"

". . . just got excited when the lights went out," Mary Rose went on, trying to figure what had happened, "and forgot this little statue was here. That's when she fell and hurt herself. And that was the bump and the moaning we heard," Mary Rose concluded triumphantly. "And then she fainted. I wonder if she hit her head."

"Well, what do we do now?"

Mary Rose was already doing it. Her searching fingers moved gently. "She did hit her head, Jo-Beth. She's got a big lump back here."

"Her right hand looks funny, too," Jo-Beth reported. "It's all swollen." She repeated her question. "What do we do now?"

"Do you remember when Daddy fell down the steps and twisted his ankle? He was knocked out, too." Jo-Beth nodded. Of course she remembered. Their mother had covered her father with a blanket and had warned them not to try to move him. "In case he's hurt his back. Never move an unconscious person," their mother had

told them. And she had put an ice pack on his leg. "To keep the swelling down."

"See if there's a bathroom or a kitchen through that door," Mary Rose instructed.

"Not me," Jo-Beth said promptly. "I'm not going into any old dark room. Not me."

"There's plenty of light from the fire."

"Sure. In here. Why don't you go?" Jo-Beth asked. You'd think they were at home, the way Mary Rose was ordering her to do this and do that.

While she was thinking, Jo-Beth looked around the room. Finally, her eyes rested on the silver candlestick. Of course! It was just the thing! She could light the candle in the fireplace. She ran over to the candle and picked it up.

"We can light this, Mary Rose," she said eagerly. "It's such a big candle, it'll burn for a long time."

"Are you *crazy?*" Mary Rose gasped. "You're not supposed to light that kind of candle! That's just for show, like the one Grandma Jenny has on the dining room table. Now I'm going to see what's in there. You can stay here till I come back."

At that moment, Vilmor Finton groaned.

"I'm coming with you," Jo-Beth said hastily. Together, the girls started to explore the room beyond the door.

"It's a kitchen," Jo-Beth said, surprised. "I didn't know they had kitchens in a library."

"Well, this isn't like a real library," Mary Rose decided. "Start looking through those drawers, Jo-Beth. See if there are any candles and matches around."

Jo-Beth thought it was kind of fun, poking through the cabinets. "Hey, I found a candlestick. Wait a minute. Here's another one."

"And I found candles and matches," Mary Rose said. Lighting two candles, Mary Rose fitted them into the candlesticks carefully and then placed them on the table.

"Now what are you doing?" Jo-Beth asked as her sister began searching through the cabinets again.

"I'm looking for plastic bags."

"Plastic bags?" Jo-Beth repeated blankly. "Plastic bags? What for?"

Mary Rose didn't answer. She had found

what she was looking for and was already opening the small freezer door at the top of the refrigerator. She removed a tray of ice cubes. Some of the cubes fell on the floor when she began to pour them into two of the bags.

"That librarian is sure going to love the way you're making a mess of her kitchen."

Still Mary Rose didn't reply. When the bags were fairly full, she tied them with two of the wire loops that were in the box with the bags.

"You've made an ice pack," Jo-Beth said. "Sometimes you're real smart, Mary Rose."

"Well, I *am* ten," Mary Rose said kindly. "Now, let's go back in and put one bag under her head, and one on her arm. You bring the candlesticks."

Mary Rose went out of the kitchen quickly, with Jo-Beth following, holding the candlesticks with her arms outstretched.

Mary Rose lifted Vilmor Finton's head gently and put the bag at the base of her neck. Then she placed the librarian's arm on the second ice pack.

"Come on," she told her sister, taking one of the candlesticks.

"Where are we going now?"

"We have to find something to cover her with," Mary Rose explained. "She has to be kept warm."

"I wish she'd move." Jo-Beth looked down at the silent form on the floor. "It's so creepy. I know she isn't exactly dead, but she isn't exactly alive, either."

"Make sure you hold the candle way out in front of you, so your clothes don't catch on fire."

The two girls walked across the room and baek into the hallway. The mynah bird, who had fallen asleep, now woke up and called after them in an anxious voice, "Say how do you do."

"How do you do. How do you do," Jo-Beth repeated rapidly. "Who are we supposed to say how do you do to?" She opened a door and held the candlestick high.

"I found the bathroom."

"Never mind the bathroom. Here's her bed-room. Help me pull the spread off the bed, Jo-Beth. We better take the blankets, too."

The girls went back along the hallway, dragging their treasures behind them.

"Watch her arm. Watch her head," Mary Rose directed as the two girls wrapped Miss Finton's body, piling the blankets and the heavy bedspread on top of her, carefully tucking them in at her sides. "There," she said, satisfied at last. "That will keep her good and warm."

"Is it almost morning? I'm getting awfully tired."

Mary Rose looked at her watch and couldn't believe what she saw. She shook the watch, then held it up against her ear.

"Has your watch stopped?"

"No. It's still going. But it says seven o'clock. That can't be right."

"Is it seven o'clock tomorrow morning already or is it seven o'clock tonight?" In a place as strange as this, Jo-Beth wouldn't be surprised if time ran on a different schedule.

"We've only been here two hours!"

"You mean we've still got another whole long night before morning?" Jo-Beth wanted to cry. "Not another whole long night!"

"It's not another one. It's the same one." She had a sudden thought. "You know what, Jo-

Beth. Let's go see what's in the refrigerator."

*

Jo-Beth was cheerful as soon as she took the first bite of chicken. "This is real good. You think she'll be mad, us eating up her food?"

"With the power off, the food would spoil anyway," Mary Rose said practically. "It would be a shame to have to throw away good food." She helped herself to a generous portion of potato salad.

In the other room, meanwhile, Vilmor Finton's eyes were now open. She had come swimming up out of her inner darkness, telling herself she had had a nightmare. Why else would she feel that she was freezing and burning at the same time? Someone had put piles of stones on her body, she had thought before she opened her eyes. Heavy stones, because she could not move. Now, fully awake, she realized that she was weighed down with blankets and her bedspread.

She sat up, shakily, pushing the covers off with her good right hand. She reached around and touched the bump on the back of her head. The pain made her take her hand away quickly.

Looking down at the floor, she saw the bag of ice cubes on which her arm had rested. Ice packs! No wonder her head and arm were numb with cold.

"Vilmor! Yoo-hoo. Vilmor!" the mynah bird greeted her. "What's your name, child?"

"Oh, go to sleep," Miss Finton said in a cross voice.

The sound of her voice brought the girls from the kitchen quickly. When Miss Finton turned around—ever so slowly, so that her head wouldn't fall off—Mary Rose and Jo-Beth were standing in the doorway, clutching half-eaten chicken legs, and staring at her with wide, interested eyes.

7.

"Now's the Time to Chase the Squirrel"

"No one is allowed on this floor," Miss Finton said sharply. "What are you doing here?" She took a deep breath, and her nostrils flared. When she did this, Miss Finton was really angry. "How dare you dress up in those clothes? And you're eating! *You're eating in those clothes!* Who let you girls in?"

Jo-Beth moved behind Mary Rose. There were so many questions. Which one were they supposed to answer first?

"She's not very nice," Jo-Beth whispered to her sister. "I don't like her."

"This is not a popularity contest," Miss Finton snapped. "It isn't necessary for you to like me." Jo-Beth's whisper had been loud enough to be heard. Miss Finton felt very irritated. Her head ached; her arm hurt; these two children had appeared out of thin air—worse, they had touched one of the displays!—and now the younger one was standing there, eating Miss Finton's food, and saying that she didn't like her.

"We saved your life," Mary Rose said, putting her arm around Jo-Beth and giving Miss Finton a defiant look. Mary Rose was scared. She didn't know what the librarian was going to do next.

"You saved my . . . oh, the blankets. And the ice packs. I suppose you were responsible for that," she told Mary Rose.

"Jo-Beth helped . . ."

"All right. You girls come and sit down and tell me what you are doing here. Then we will go downstairs and you will take those dresses off and put on your own clothes."

Miss Finton settled comfortably on the sofa. She was beginning to feel a little better. The pain in the back of her head was not so strong, although the bump was still tender to the touch. And there was only a dull ache in her sprained wrist. In a moment, she would get the elastic bandage from the bathroom cabinet and wrap it around her wrist. Right now she wanted to know who the girls were and how they had found their way into the closed library.

Mary Rose started, with Jo-Beth interrupting along the way to get the facts straight.

"Well. If that doesn't beat buttered parsnips!" Vilmor Finton declared when the girls had finished telling her about their adventures in the library up until the time they had found her on the floor.

Jo-Beth sent her sister an anxious glance. What a strange thing to say. What was a parsnip, anyway? It sounded like a little animal with short sharp claws and tiny beady eyes. But why, Jo-Beth wondered, would anyone want to butter it?

Earlier, when Jo-Beth had explained about the emergency that had brought them to the library, Miss Finton had exclaimed, "That must have been your father at the door. And I gave him hail and farewell so fast the poor man left before he got here."

Jo-Beth had tried to interrupt, to add that her

61

father was Last-Minute Harry, but Mary Rose had just rushed on with the story. She had reached the part where they had dressed up in the clothing they found in the kid hack room and had sat on a bench with the dolls behind them. She just kept on talking and talking, and Jo-Beth couldn't get a word in edgewise.

But now Mary Rose had finished at last.

"Why couldn't you hear us talking and walking around downstairs?" Mary Rose now asked. She toasted a marshmallow in the fire, waiting until it was crisp and golden before popping it into her mouth. She and Jo-Beth had been eating steadily since they had discovered the kitchen.

"I was upstairs."

"You mean there's another floor over this one?" Jo-Beth's eyes opened wide. "This house must be bigger than a castle."

"It's a mansion," Mary Rose corrected her sister. "That's what they used to call all the big old houses—mansions."

"How can this be a mansion and a library, too?" Jo-Beth snatched the last marshmallow from the box. That made it even, five for Mary Rose and five for herself. Miss Finton had turned them down. "They don't sit well on my stomach," Miss Finton had announced. Jo-Beth had closed her eyes and tried to imagine a row of toasted marshmallows with sticklike legs and arms, sitting on Miss Finton's stomach, slipping and sliding because they couldn't sit well. She had opened her eyes in a hurry, though, when she thought Mary Rose was trying to sneak the last marshmallow.

"There were no library branches in this whole neighborhood, and certainly nothing that was special just for children. And here was I, all alone and with rooms to spare. I made the offer to turn the first floor over to the library and before you could say coffee grows in a white oak tree, they agreed. And we've both been here a long time." Miss Finton stared at the fire. "But now they've built a fine modern library, and they won't be using this house anymore." After a moment, she added, her eyes snapping, "They say we have to move with the times."

"Who are 'they'?" Jo-Beth asked, curiously.

Mary Rose, studying Miss Finton's angry face, changed the subject quickly. "Do you think the blizzard is almost over? Do you think the power will come back on soon?"

"Blizzard? What blizzard?" Miss Finton couldn't believe all the things she was hearing. How long had she been lying on the floor?

"That's what the operator said. On the phone. It's dead," Mary Rose told Miss Finton, who had automatically started to reach for the telephone near the sofa.

"I have a small radio in the kitchen that works on batteries. I'll get it and see if we can find out the latest news about the weather."

"You'd better let me go," Mary Rose began, but Miss Finton was already on her feet.

"I'm not the queen, and I'll do it for myself, thank you very much." She went marching off to the kitchen. Over her shoulder, she instructed Mary Rose to get the elastic bandage from the bathroom cabinet.

Jo-Beth edged closer to her sister. "I'll go with you. I don't want to stay here with her by myself. She says the queerest things. I don't know what she means half the time she's talking."

"A lot of grownups talk funny, Jo-Beth. Come on, if you're coming."

When the two girls came back with the bandage, Miss Finton was already sitting on the sofa again. Mary Rose helped Miss Finton wind the bandage around her swollen wrist, and Jo-Beth turned the radio on. A voice came leaping out at them. The reporter was so excited, all his sentences sounded as if they ended in exclamation marks.

> ... the worst storm in our history. It's still snowing heavily; power is out in many parts of the city.
>
> Travelers have been forced to find shelter in schools and other public buildings. Cars have been abandoned in the streets. Already many cars have been completely covered by the drifting snow.

"I warned Daddy the snow would cover the car and we would freeze to death," Jo-Beth announced. "I told him that would happen."

"Well, you didn't freeze to death. So don't be so dramatic, Jo-Beth. We're probably warmer than Daddy is right now."

Miss Finton held up a finger for silence. She

wanted to hear what else the reporter had to say.

> ... accidents. People are urged not to go out unless
> it is absolutely necessary. Already there have been
> many reports of serious problems—a house burning
> on the far Eastside of town and fire engines unable
> to reach the flaming structure. And the father of two
> small girls who mysteriously disappeared from their
> car parked on the near Northside early this evening
> now fears foul play.

"Foul play! That's us!" Jo-Beth was excited. "I wonder if they're showing our pictures on TV. I hope they didn't show my school picture."

"Foul play!" Miss Finton repeated in a hollow voice. "Oh, that poor, poor man. I shall never forgive myself for turning him away. Never."

"That's silly," Mary Rose said sensibly. "You didn't know. Why, the last thing Daddy said to us was to keep the doors locked and not talk to any strangers. Anyway, we're perfectly all right."

"But Daddy doesn't know that." Another thought struck Jo-Beth. "I wonder if Mommy knows. Maybe she doesn't even care, now that she's having this new baby and all," she added.

"Don't pay any attention to Jo-Beth. Everything's like a play on the stage to her."

"Turn the radio off," Miss Finton instructed, "and try the phone again. Maybe they've repaired the lines."

Mary Rose obligingly lifted the receiver of the phone. "It's still out of order."

Jo-Beth was thinking again about having her picture shown on TV. "I wish they could show us in these clothes. Wouldn't Daddy be surprised?"

Miss Finton sat up straight. "Weevily wheat!" She had almost forgotten. She struggled to her feet. "You girls bring the candles."

"Where are we going?" Mary Rose asked.

"Downstairs. To the kid hack display. You are going to remove those dresses and put your own things on, right now."

"I hate it down there. It's dark and scary," Jo-Beth protested.

"Can't we change when it gets light again?" Mary Rose didn't want to go downstairs, either. Why leave this cozy room, with its crackling fire, and cheerful, pleasant warmth?

"Now's the time to chase the squirrel," Miss Finton insisted. "There's nothing to be afraid of. Come along."

There was no arguing with Miss Finton. Even the mynah bird, taking interest in their movements, flew down after them.

Jo-Beth tried not to look at the shadows they were casting on the wall as they went down the steps, but her eyes were drawn to them again

and again. The strange figures on the wall bobbed up and down; they stretched high and long, then vanished at the stair landing, only to bob up again below. Since the girls were wearing long, old-fashioned dresses, their shadows seemed to rise up from the base of the floor as if they were growing right out of the wood.

She was almost glad to reach the kid hack room. Silently, the two girls undressed, and began to put on their own clothes.

Suddenly Jo-Beth, who had glanced toward the large center room, caught her breath.

"What's the matter now?" Mary Rose demanded. Jo-Beth shook her head, and pointed a shaking finger.

There, in the large room, papers were swirling up from Miss Finton's desk, moving in circles, a dipping, gliding, silent dance in the air.

8.

When
the Banshee
Cries

"I want to go home!" Jo-Beth wailed, when she could speak again. "I don't like it here. This place is haunted."

Mary Rose nodded. That ghostly movement of the papers was frightening. She wished there was some place they could hide until daylight came.

"The basement door!" Miss Finton exclaimed. "It must have blown open somehow." She took the candlestick away from Jo-Beth. "You girls can stay here, or come with me. I'm going to investigate."

The girls rushed to her side as she began to leave the room. They felt that if they looked back, they would see the figures in the kid hack

70

turning to stare after them. Anything was better than that.

"She's awfully bossy," Jo-Beth whispered to her sister. "I bet she doesn't even like kids."

"I don't like children who handle displays and take things that don't belong to them," Miss Finton snapped. "Or children who called her bossy, either," Jo-Beth thought, sighing.

Miss Finton led them directly to the basement door, which was swinging back and forth.

"Ghosts!" Miss Finton muttered. She examined the door. "The lock doesn't catch. I'll have to have it fixed."

"It's so cold." Mary Rose shivered. "Why is it so cold?"

A stream of chilly air was coming up from the basement.

"There must be a window open down there. Come along, girls. Come along," she repeated, as the girls held back. "We'll need the light from both candles." Miss Finton was already on her way down the steps, walking very carefully. Mary Rose followed, holding one hand in front of the candle to keep it from blowing out. That meant Jo-Beth had to walk last again. She wished there was some way she could go down the steps backward. It would be better to look into the darkness rather than have it creep up behind her.

They were almost at the bottom of the stairway when Miss Finton said, "I hear a cat."

"That's not a cat," Jo-Beth said in a faint voice. "It's a banshee."

"A what?" Mary Rose cried.

"A banshee." Jo-Beth nodded her head. She had just finished reading a book of Irish fairy tales. "Don't you even know what a banshee is? That's a spirit that cries under a window. When the banshee cries like that, it means someone is going to die."

The candle trembled in Mary Rose's hand. "You just quit it, Jo-Beth. You just quit it right now. You're only trying to scare me."

"There are no banshees in this house." Miss Finton's voice was firm. One look at her face, and the girls could see that Miss Finton wouldn't allow such a thing in her library. "I declare! I've never met anyone as jumpy as you.

Everything has a perfectly reasonable explanation. You should try to control your imagination, young lady."

Miss Finton's head had begun to throb again, and her swollen wrist ached. She was sorry she had snapped at Jo-Beth, but everything seemed to be out of control. Vilmor Finton didn't like things to be out of control. It was unsettling.

"It's this spooky old house. It's worse than the wax museum! And I thought *that* was scary. I wouldn't be afraid to go there now. Not after being here."

"The very idea!" Miss Finton was insulted. "This happens to be a lovely old house."

"Don't mind my sister." Mary Rose was trying to soothe the librarian's feelings, but Miss Finton's only reply was, "Watch this last step. It's broken."

She held her candle high so the girls could see the step. They could also peer at the basement, which seemed to go on and on until it vanished in the darkness.

"Why is everything so big in this house?" Jo-Beth complained.

"It was the way Grandfather Finton built . . . ohhhhhhh!"

Jo-Beth had just bumped against her bandaged wrist. For a moment, Miss Finton felt so sick from the pain that she almost dropped the candle.

"There it goes again!" Jo-Beth ran back up a few steps and stopped.

Mary Rose shivered. She could feel icy air all around her. Could Jo-Beth be right? Was there such a thing as a banshee?

"Look." Miss Finton was pointing at a window high up on a wall of the basement. "There's your banshee."

"Oh, the poor little thing. Look, Jo-Beth. It *is* a cat, and he's half in and half out of the window. He must have tried to get in out of the blizzard and the window closed down on him. Oh, the poor little thing. No wonder he's crying."

"And that accounts for the air that moved the papers around upstairs," Miss Finton added. "And that's what I mean about too much imagination."

Jo-Beth was quiet. "It's easy to be smart *after*

you know the facts," she thought, but Mary
Rose had been scared, too, she was sure. And
Miss Finton must have been scared as well, even
if she pretended otherwise.

"There's a ladder behind the steps, Mary
Rose. You and Jo-Beth pull it over to the window. Be careful when you reach for the cat. And
pull the window shut and lock it."

Miss Finton was still giving advice when Mary Rose climbed the ladder. She pushed at the window and pulled the cat free. As she carried the shivering animal down, she murmured softly in its ear. She handed the cat to Jo-Beth who cuddled it against her body to warm it.

"You and your banshees," Mary Rose said, after she locked the window and came down. "You almost had me believing you."

Jo-Beth ran her hand over the cat's fur.

"It could have been a banshee," she told herself stubbornly. In a house like this, anything was possible. But she kept her thoughts to herself.

9.

"Madame Morgana Sees All and Knows All"

"Now that we've rescued the cat," Miss Finton said, "we might just as well get back upstairs to the fire. The poor thing needs warming."

"I wish someone would rescue us," Jo-Beth mourned. "Only if *we* screamed, nobody would hear us."

"Shipwrecked sailors send up flares." Mary Rose had seen that once in a movie on TV.

"Flares," Miss Finton said, in a strange voice. "Rockets! Of course. We'll shoot off rockets!"

The two girls looked at each other. Jo-Beth huddled against her sister.

"There she goes again," she whispered.

"Rockets?" Mary Rose repeated. "We'll shoot off *rockets?*"

"What kind of rockets?" Jo-Beth squeezed the cat so hard it gave a protesting cry.

"Don't you girls know what rockets are?" Miss Finton demanded. "Roman candles! Fireworks! Fourth of July! Whisshhhh!" She waved her good arm in the air. "Beautiful colors exploding in the sky." She looked up at the ceiling, and the girls did, too, almost expecting to see fireworks. "The trick now is," Miss Finton said in a somewhat doubtful voice, "finding them down here. We'll just have to pick our way around things very carefully. You girls will have to open a few boxes for me."

She began to walk deeper into the basement. Mary Rose followed quickly; Jo-Beth put the cat down and went after them.

"Now mind you don't bump into the animals," Miss Finton warned.

The sisters stopped walking. Animals in the basement? What kind of animals?

"What kind of animals?" Jo-Beth whispered. "I think I'm going to faint. I am. I'm going to faint." She squeezed her eyelids shut.

"Children don't faint. Grownups faint. Anyway, take a look." Mary Rose held her candle high. She had already taken a peek. "Come on. Open your eyes."

When Jo-Beth took a chance and opened her eyes, she saw the animals directly to her left. There were four of them—a lion with its head thrown back, a snarling tiger, a gentle-eyed llama, and a large graceful swan. All were made of wood; all had once been brightly painted. But all the animals were now faded and peeling in spots.

"From a merry-go-round," Miss Finton told them. "My grandfather was a collector. He loved wooden figures. The house is full of them. I think the box I'm looking for is behind the hurdy-gurdy. Come along."

Rush. Rush. Rush. That was Miss Finton. Jo-Beth wished she wouldn't hurry them so. She wanted to stroke the merry-go-round animals, especially the tiger. He was so fierce and scary it gave Jo-Beth a delicious cold feeling right down her spine.

"What's a hurdy-gurdy?" Mary Rose asked.

"A hurdy-gurdy? Why, that's a hand organ. What we used to call a barrel organ. A man used to wheel one of these things around on the city streets. He'd stop where he saw a lot of people and he'd turn this handle. See?" Miss Finton cranked the handle and a tune stumbled out. It sounded rusty and tired and as if some of the notes were missing. "When I was a little girl, my father took me to New York one time. We saw the hurdy-gurdy man, and children dancing in the street while he kept turning the handle on the organ. Even some of the women danced, too. Sometimes the hurdy-gurdy man had a monkey with him, dressed up in a little red suit and a funny little hat. When the man stopped playing, the monkey would come around and hold out his cap and people would drop money into it. Then he'd bring it back to the hurdy-gurdy man."

"I like that." Mary Rose laughed. "Why don't they do that anymore?"

"Old fashioned. Like the dresses you put on. And this house. I wish we had more light down here." Miss Finton put out her hand and touched a glass case sitting on a high box. While the girls walked around the hurdy-gurdy, admiring its large red-spoked wheels, and trying to turn the handle, Miss Finton picked up a coin from beside the glass case and dropped it into a slot.

Flashing lights that flickered on and off—white and purple and red—lit up the head and arms and bright green blouse of a waxen-faced woman with large, black, glaring eyes. Only the upper half of her body could be seen. She had coal-black hair, tightly pulled back, long, glittering earrings, and a spot of bright red on each cheek. Now her tight lips parted; she spoke. She turned her head and stared right at Mary Rose and Jo-Beth. "Put another penny in," she commanded, "and I will tell your fortune."

"Kilamakrankie!" Miss Finton swore. "I didn't mean to startle you. That's Madame Morgana. She tells fortunes. I just thought we could use some more light in here. She runs on batteries."

It was lighter, but the girls didn't feel braver.

"It was better in the dark," Jo-Beth said.

"Well, I've got to feed her pennies till I find the rockets." She dropped another coin in and walked around Madame Morgana. "Come along, Mary Rose. I'm sure I've found it. You'll have to get it open for me."

Mary Rose followed Miss Finton, but she kept
staring over her shoulder at Madame Morgana,
whose arms were moving one way while her
head was turning another in tiny, jerky motions.
Madame Morgana picked up a card and slipped
it into a small opening under the glass. "This is
your fortune," her creaky voice told Jo-Beth,
who was standing and staring up at the strange

figure, watching her with wide eyes, her mouth open in surprise. "Read it and believe. Madame Morgana sees all and knows all."

The card came out. As Jo-Beth reached up to take it, the lights in the glass case went out, but Jo-Beth could still see her dimly in the light of the candles.

"Put another penny in," Miss Finton called. "I think Mary Rose and I have found the rockets."

"Never mind," Mary Rose shouted hastily. "It's the right box. We don't need Madame Morgana anymore."

Jo-Beth looked down at the card in her hand.

Strange things will happen
to you in a place of mystery. You will
fear for your life, but you will be
saved. Tell no one of your adventures.
They will not believe you.

Jo-Beth stared up at Madame Morgana again in amazement. How could a wooden figure— and only half of one, at that—have known about all the things that had happened to her and Mary Rose?

Going back upstairs, Jo-Beth was very thoughtful. While Miss Finton examined the rockets when they were back on the second floor, Jo-Beth told her sister, "This isn't a house. It's a museum. I'll tell you one thing, Mary Rose. If we ever get out of here—alive, I mean—I'm never ever in my whole life going to tell people about this place."

"Why not? That's so silly. People will want to know, won't they? Where we've been all this time, and all?"

Jo-Beth shook her head stubbornly.

"I'm not going to say one word." She looked up at the mynah bird, who had flown back to its cage some time ago. It had been dozing when they had come back to the room. Now it said sleepily. "Off with their heads!"

"Not one word. To anybody. About anything," Jo-Beth added firmly.

10.

"Black the Boots and Make Them Shine"

Jo-Beth was beginning to feel as if she had spent hours walking up and down and around this big old house. She was tired. The cat was, too, she thought. It had followed them upstairs, studied the mynah bird with narrow eyes, and then had leaped up on the sofa. Curling itself cozily in one of the blankets, it promptly went to sleep.

That's what Jo-Beth wanted to do, too—lie down on a soft bed, pull a blanket up around her face, and not wake up until the sun came up in the morning.

"Couldn't we shoot off the rockets tomorrow?" she asked hopefully. "Aunt Madge won't mind if we don't get to her house until tomorrow. Nobody likes visitors at night anyway," she added.

"Fiddlesticks," Miss Finton replied. "We've got to get a message out somehow and let your parents know you girls are safe. Off we go. Mind how you carry that box upstairs, Mary Rose. I'll light the way ahead of you and Jo-Beth can walk right behind you."

"There it goes again," Jo-Beth thought resentfully. "Just because I'm the youngest one here, I have to come trailing behind everybody. Well, once the baby is here—if he isn't here already—I won't be the youngest anymore. It will be my turn to tell somebody what to do, and he'll have to listen." She felt better about the baby somehow. She'd have somebody to boss around . . .

"Will you watch what you're doing!" Mary Rose yelled. "You trying to set me on fire or something? Keep that candle away from my hair."

"How far up do these steps go?" Jo-Beth complained. "It's like climbing a mountain."

From the basement to the third floor was exhausting, Miss Finton admitted, but she fairly flew up all the steps just the same. "I'm half mountain goat," she added.

"Don't pay any attention to Jo-Beth," Mary

Rose puffed—the box kept getting heavier the higher they went—"she always wants to know if we're there yet."

"Well, we are there." Miss Finton led the way. "Let's put the box down here, beside this window. It has a good solid windowsill. We'll need something solid as a base for shooting off the rockets."

"Like a launching pad for a rocket to the moon." Mary Rose laughed. She put the box down and looked around. She could see all kinds of different-shaped objects, but she couldn't tell what they were. "What's up here, anyway?"

"The car flasher." Miss Finton suddenly remembered. "It's in the storage closet. Bring your candles, girls."

Mary Rose and Jo-Beth kept close to her as she walked across the huge room.

"I knew it. There it sits, up on the shelf. I'll hand it down to you, Mary Rose. There you go. Careful, now."

Miss Finton clicked on a small switch. A strong red light came on at once. It went round and round, lighting up different figures near by. "My safety emergency lantern. Always take it with me in the car when I travel. I've never seen such a fidgety child," she said to Mary Rose. Jo-Beth *was* fidgeting—each time a new figure was caught in the eery red glow, Jo-Beth jumped.

"What kind of place is this?" she asked once again.

"Bring your candles over here. Let me show you something." Miss Finton watched the expressions on the faces of the two girls when they recognized two figures up on a platform. Raggedy Ann and Raggedy Andy were sitting on two large chairs. They were smiling at a strange-looking creature, with striped arms and a striped band around his long round head, who was holding a dish of cookies in his hands.

"Mr. Cookie!" Jo-Beth shouted. "He's from *Raggedy Ann in Cookie Land.* I have that book."

"Do you know these people?" Miss Finton asked, walking to the next display. There was the figure of a man, wearing a crown on his head, and a long purple robe trimmed with fur, sitting at a table counting money. Near him, a lady with a tall cone-shaped hat, on top of which perched a tiny crown, was sitting on a throne, eating a slice of bread. On the floor beside her a bottle marked HONEY was tipped over on its side. On the edge of this platform, a figure dressed in a uniform with a tiny white frilly apron was hanging clothes on a line. A bird was pulling at her nose.

Mary Rose didn't even have to look at the card beside the platform. She began to sing:

> *The king was in his counting-house,*
> *Counting out his money;*
> *The queen was in the parlor,*
> *Eating bread and honey;*
> *The maid was in the garden,*
> *Hanging out the clothes*
> *When down came a blackbird*
> *And pecked off her nose.*

"What else is up here?" Jo-Beth asked eagerly.

"Do you remember the Cowardly Lion? And the Straw Man? And the Tin Man?" Miss Finton pointed to a far corner of the room. "There they all are—skipping down the Yellow Brick Road."

"What about the Wicked Witch of the West? I liked her best. She was so mean." Mary Rose shivered.

"We have two scenes set up from *The Wizard of Oz*. That's still a very popular book," Miss Finton explained.

"I never saw a house like this," Mary Rose exclaimed.

"I told you my grandfather was a collector. This used to be the ballroom, but Grandfather collected so many things, this became a big storage area, just like the basement. I don't know what's going to happen to it all when this old house is torn down some day." Miss Finton's voice became husky. "I grew up with these storybook people."

"You could sell them," Mary Rose said.

"Nobody wants stuff like this anymore. They'd make good firewood, I guess." She brushed tears from her eyes angrily. "Well, black the boots and make them shine," she went on in a fierce tone. "Talking isn't doing. And we're up here to do. To the window, girls. Let's get those rockets in the air."

Jo-Beth followed them slowly. She was thinking hard. There must be something Miss Finton could do with this collection. Storybook people shouldn't become firewood. That wasn't right.

She had said something to her sister earlier ... a word she had used ... What was it? Why couldn't she remember?

"Never mind," she told herself as she approached the window. With everything that had happened since they had come to the library, it was a wonder she still knew her own name.

That word would come back to her. And when it did, she had a feeling she'd be able to help Miss Finton.

11.

Fireworks
in the
Snow

"Can you shoot off fireworks when it's snow-ing?" Mary Rose seemed doubtful.

"We'll soon find out, won't we?" Miss Finton opened the window slowly. Fortunately, the wind was blowing from the north; the window was on the south side of the house and protected by the overhang of the roof. There was very little snow on the window ledge. "I think it's stopped." Miss Finton put her hand out. "No, it's still snowing. But it seems to have let up a bit." She began to fit the stand for the rockets into the window brackets. "My grandfather had this specially made. We used to come upstairs every Fourth of July, and he put on a whiz-bang show. You could see the fireworks for miles around. Of course, he never let us children handle the fireworks. Too dangerous, he said."

Mary Rose had been about to ask if she could shoot off the Roman candles, but wisely she said nothing. Miss Finton was already telling the girls to go and watch from another window close by. "Just in case something happens," she said bravely.

The first two Roman candles fizzled and dropped below, disappearing into a snow bank. The next few flared briefly and died.

"I knew they wouldn't work." Mary Rose was disappointed. She was also tired and feeling a little cranky. It was now past midnight, long after her usual bedtime. Like Jo-Beth, right now all she wanted to do was lie down and go to sleep.

"Where's the spirit that won the West?" Miss Finton demanded. "We'll stay here until the last rocket goes up."

Jo-Beth sighed. "How many are left?"

Miss Finton didn't reply; she had just sent another rocket into the air. It made a series of booming noises, then the sky lit up in a shower

of sparkling reds and yellows. The rocket that
followed exploded into a fine sprinkle of greens
and blues.

"Hal-loo! Hal-lay!" Miss Finton crowed.
"That made the old woman go flippety flop!"

"Shoot the rest of them." Jo-Beth was eager
now to see more fireworks. The bright colors
were beautiful and exciting against the dark,

brooding sky. Unfortunately, the few Roman candles that were left did not go off.

The girls pressed their faces against the windowpane, staring hopefully at the street. Everything remained silent. Nothing moved. It was as if everyone in the world had vanished. The snow, which had appeared to stop, was now coming down harder than ever. The wind picked it up and piled it against every object in its path.

Miss Finton clicked off the red safety lantern. Their candles had burned so low they were in danger of going out. Quietly, all three went back downstairs to the second floor. No one spoke— what was there to say?

Miss Finton built up the fire in the fireplace with Mary Rose's help. The girls decided they would sleep on the floor in front of the fireplace; it was warm and cheery and lifted their spirits a little. Miss Finton stretched out on the sofa.

"Never mind, girls," she called. "Tomorrow is another day." She received no reply; both girls were fast asleep.

12.

Last-Minute Harry to the Rescue

"Turn the lights out. They're shining right in my eyes," Jo-Beth complained sleepily. Suddenly she came wide awake. She shook Mary Rose. "The lights! The lights are back on!"

Miss Finton sat up on the sofa as Mary Rose yawned and rubbed her nose.

"The power's back," Jo-Beth said, excited. "And look! The sun is shining. It's morning!"

"Switch the TV on," Miss Finton commanded. "Let's see if we can get the latest news about the blizzard."

A picture came on at once. A reporter, clutching a microphone and speaking rapidly, sounded as if he couldn't believe his own words.

I'm standing in the heart of downtown Indianapolis on what is usually a working day. Normally, cars would be bumper to bumper. But as you can see, the streets are deserted for miles. Everything is closed up tight.

Although it has now stopped snowing, the streets are impassable. Owners of four-wheel drive trucks and vans are being asked to help the city in rescue operations. The police ask that everyone else stay home. Traveling is extremely dangerous because of drifts and icy roads.

"I guess that means no one will be coming to get us," Mary Rose mourned.

"Shhhh! They're back in the studio," Miss Finton said. "Listen."

. . . and there have been some scattered reports of fireworks last night which appeared to be coming from Pennsylvania Street on the near Northside. Police are investigating . . .

"Shut that thing off," Miss Finton ordered. "If the phone is working, I want to make a call."

The phone was in good order. Miss Finton called the police department. She talked and explained and listened, and talked and explained again. When she hung up, she was smiling.

"It will take a while for the rescue van to get here. But at least now your father knows where you are, and that you're safe. Poor man. He spent the night at the police station waiting for news about you. He's calling your mother at once. And by the way, girls. You have a new baby brother. His name is Harry Two."

"I knew it would be a boy," Jo-Beth insisted, but somehow it didn't seem to bother her much this morning. She ran over to the birdcage and removed the cover. "It's morning. Wake up."

The mynah bird lifted its head, looked about, and said chattily, "What's your name, child?" and then began to preen its feathers.

On the sofa, the cat licked its paws and carefully washed its face. Then it meowed for food.

"Come along, little Banshee," Miss Finton said, picking up the cat. "We'll give you a saucer of milk. Would you girls like some hot chocolate for breakfast?"

After they were finished eating, Miss Finton suggested that the two sisters explore the house. "With the lights on, I think you'll find it very interesting, and not the least bit scary."

When the girls came back from their tour,

they were bubbling with excitement. Miss Finton was back on the sofa, watching the cat, who was stretched out before the fire.

"Still think this is like a wax museum?" she asked.

That was the word Jo-Beth had been trying to remember. "That's it!" she shouted. "That's it!"

"Are you starting in again?" Mary Rose wondered. "Haven't we had enough?"

"You don't understand. That's what this library really is—a museum." Jo-Beth was so excited, she began to talk faster and faster. "A storybook museum. Wouldn't that be wonderful? You know how we're always going on field trips, Mary Rose. To the Children's Museum. And the Art Museum. And to the Fort. Suppose there was a storybook museum, too. There could be books here, that kids could buy, telling all about the different displays . . ."

"What a neat idea!" Mary Rose was impressed. This was one time she really had to admire her sister's imagination.

Jo-Beth turned to Miss Finton, her eyes sparkling. "And you said they would make good firewood, all these beautiful storybook people."

"It's not that easy," Miss Finton objected. "You can't start a museum just like that. It would take money. And people to run it . . ."

"You're here," Mary Rose interrupted.

"Mary Rose is right. You could be the caretaker. And guide . . ."

"The Finton Storybook Museum," Mary Rose said dreamily. "What a really neat idea!"

"It's out of the question . . ."

"Couldn't you at least talk to someone about it? Some grownup?" Jo-Beth pleaded.

"Well, I do have some good friends in the community. I suppose we could start a campaign to raise funds. People want to see this city grow. Nothing may come of it, of course . . ."

"But you'll try. You'll try!"

When Miss Finton nodded, Jo-Beth shouted, "Hooray!" then ran over and hugged her. "I do love this house. And I love you. You're funny, but you're nice."

"Jo-Beth!" Mary Rose was shocked, but Miss Finton smiled.

"Never you mind, child. I am funny. That happens to people who live alone sometimes. But I can't think of a nicer way to start the day

than to be told that you're nice and someone loves you. Thank you, Jo-Beth."

Mary Rose ran to the window. "I think I heard a car." She rubbed the pane clear. "There's a truck ... it looks like an army truck. And there's a man with a camera. Hey! There's Daddy. There's Daddy!" She tried to get the window open, then followed Jo-Beth, who was already racing down the steps.

Miss Finton came right behind them with the keys in her hand. She reached the door just as Mr. Onetree came bounding up on to the porch. He pounded impatiently on the glass. "Open up! Open up in there!" The cameraman was busily filming the whole scene.

Miss Finton unlocked the inner door. Then she opened the outer door. Mr. Onetree rushed in and hugged the two girls. He was laughing and crying and scolding them all at the same time. He started to say something to Miss Finton but when he saw her bandaged arm and the guilty look on her face, he changed his mind.

"Get your snow jackets and let's go," Mr. Onetree said.

"You, too, ma'am," a policeman said. He had just come up the front steps. "Bundle up warm."

Miss Finton said she was fine, but the policeman insisted. "They said on the phone that you were hurt. Can't leave you here alone. It's not safe."

"But Duchess. And little Banshee," she protested.

102

"That's her mynah bird. And the cat that came in out of the storm," Jo-Beth explained.

"We'll bring you back, ma'am. After the doctor's looked at you."

The girls helped Miss Finton put on her coat and boots. The policeman held her firmly so she wouldn't slip on the icy sidewalk.

As they left, the cameraman took one last picture. It was of the sign in the window that Jo-Beth had printed and then forgotten:

HELP! I'M A PRISONER IN THE LIBERRY

Afterword

There is no Finton Storybook Museum in Indianapolis, but once there was an old mansion, on Meridian Street, called the Rauh Memorial Library. This writer and her young daughter were frequent visitors to that lovely home. It was not so big as the house in this story, but it looked very grand and large to the child. The Rauh Memorial Library was torn down, to make room for the new Children's Museum, said to be the largest in the world.

There was a blizzard in Indianapolis, the worst blizzard in the city's history.

Like many others, this writer could not get out during that blizzard, but her thoughts could escape. She remembered the Rauh Memorial Library and the pleasant hours spent there. From that storm and the memories came this story.

There are other mansions in Indianapolis that have become museums. Perhaps, some day, there will be a Storybook Museum, too!